Pinkerton, Behave!

Story and pictures by

STEVEN KELLOGG

Dial Books for Young Readers
New York

Published by
Dial Books for Young Readers
2 Park Avenue
New York, New York 10016

Copyright © 1979 by Steven Kellogg
Typography by Jane Byers Bierhorst
Printed in Hong Kong by South China Printing Co.
COBE
6 8 10 12 14 15 13 11 9 7 5

Library of Congress Cataloging in Publication Data

Kellogg, Steven.
Pinkerton, behave.

Summary/His behavior may be rather unconventional,
but Pinkerton, the dog, proves it doesn't really matter.
[1. Dogs—Fiction] I. Title.
PZ7.K292Pi [E] 78-31794
ISBN 0-8037-6573-8/ISBN 0-8037-6575-4/(lib. bdg.)

The process art consists of black line-drawings, black halftones,
and full-color washes. The black line is prepared and
photographed separately for greater sharpness and contrast.
The full-color washes and the black halftones are
prepared with ink, crayons, and paints on the reverse side
of the black line-drawing. They are then camera-separated and
reproduced as red, blue, yellow, and black halftones.

For Helen,
my best friend and
the person who chose
the Great Pinkerton

Every new puppy has to learn to behave.
First I'll teach Pinkerton to come when he's called.

Come!

He can learn to bring us the newspaper.

Fetch!

From now on *I'll* fetch the newspaper.

But it's important for him to defend the house if a burglar comes.

We'll pretend this dummy is a burglar.

Get the burglar, Pinkerton!

I think we need some professional help.
Pinkerton will have to go to obedience school.

When this poor creature sees how well the other dogs behave, he will understand what we expect of him.

We begin with a simple command. Come.

COME! COME! COME!

We cannot hold back the entire class for one confused student.
On to the next lesson!

Every dog must fetch the evening paper.

Fetch, you fleabrain, FETCH!

Our next lesson is a most important one.
Get the burglar!

Pinkerton sets a poor example for the rest of the class.
Unless he shows some improvement, he will be dismissed.

We will now review all that we have learned.
Dogs! Pay attention!

COME!

FETCH!

OUT! OUT! OUT! OUT!

Mom, you and Pinkerton look pretty tired.
Why don't you go to bed and get a good night's rest?

Pleasant dreams, Pinkerton.

This is a stickup, lady. Don't move, or I'll blast you and your silly hound to chicken powder.

I warned you, lady.

Pinkerton! Fetch!

GRRRRRRRRRRR

Pinkerton! Come!

Pinkerton, I'm a burglar.

I love you, Pinkerton.